❦ BOOK REVIEW

This gentle tale about the meaning and
responsibilities of friendship is intensified by
the brilliant illustrations.

from CHICAGO SUNDAY SUN-STANDARD

Weekly Reader Children's Book Club presents

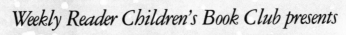

BEANY
and
SCAMP

Story by Lisa Bassett
Pictures by Jeni Bassett

DODD, MEAD, & COMPANY • New York

To Joe Ann Daly
—LB and JB

This book is a presentation of Weekly Reader Books
Weekly Reader Books offers book clubs for children
from preschool through high school. For further information
write to: **Weekly Reader Books,**
4343 Equity Drive, Columbus, Ohio 43228.
Published by arrangement with Dodd, Mead, & Company.
Weekly Reader is a trademark of Field Publications.
Printed in the United States of America.

Text copyright © 1987 by Lisa Bassett
Illustrations copyright © 1987 by Jeni Bassett

Library of Congress Cataloging-in-Publication Data

Bassett, Lisa.
  Beany and Scamp.

  Summary: Just as Beany Bear is ready for his long
winter's nap, friend Scamp Squirrel asks his help in
searching for his misplaced winter nut supply.
  [1. Bears—Fiction.   2. Squirrels—Fiction]   I.
Bassett, Jeni, ill.   II. Title.
PZ7.B2933Be   1987   [E]   86-13502
ISBN 0-396-08822-8

When the first snow fell, Beany Bear knew it was
time for his long winter's nap. He put extra
blankets on his bed and plumped up his pillow.
Then he went to say good-bye to his friend,
Scamp Squirrel.

As Beany came to Scamp's doorstep
and reached up to ring the bell,
the door suddenly flew open.
Scamp rushed out, bumped into
Beany, and fell back through
the doorway.

"Beany! I was just going out to look
for you," cried Scamp.
"And here you are right on my doorstep.
Come in, come in!
I have big plans for us today."

"But, Scamp," said Beany, squeezing inside, "it is time for me to go to bed for the winter."

"I will miss you," said Scamp sadly. "Especially today. I thought we could go together."

"Go where?" asked Beany.

"Hunting for my nuts," exclaimed Scamp. "It is
time for me to find the nuts I buried this fall.
I will not have any food for the winter
without nuts."

"I cannot leave you without food," said Beany.
"But... but how long will it take to find
your nuts? Last year ..."

"Forget last year," said Scamp hastily. "This year we will find my nuts in no time."

"Oh, I am glad you remember where you hid them," said Beany.

"But I *don't* remember," said Scamp.

"How are we going to find them?"

"Just look," cried Scamp, pulling a crumpled
piece of paper from his coat pocket.

"Have you ever seen anything as clever as *this*?"

"Well, I'm not sure," said Beany. "What is it?"

"A map!" cried Scamp. "Last fall I put all my
nuts in one place, so it would not take so long
to find them all. Then I drew a map to lead me
to them. All we have to do is follow the map.
We will be like pirates looking for buried treasure."

"It doesn't look exactly like a pirate's map,"

said Beany. "Why is the paper all purple?"

"Because I spilled a bottle of blueberry juice

on it," said Scamp.

"I think the juice blurred the lines," said Beany.

"Oh, you are right. I will put in more lines

to tidy it up," said Scamp.

He scribbled over the purple spots.

"Now, as you can easily see,

we start right here and follow the lines

until we come to the end, here.

That is where we will find my nuts."

Scamp was pointing to a square with the

word NUTS written inside.

"What does the square mean?" asked Beany.
"I wish I could remember, but then we would
not need the map," said Scamp. "We will
find out what it means when we get there.
Those nuts are hidden in a very clever place
this year, and it is all right here on the map."
Beany tried to keep from yawning. He had
a feeling that it would be a long time
before he went to bed.

"I will carry the map," said Scamp,
"and you can carry the shovel."

He trotted out the door into the frosty
woods, while Beany got the shovel out of
the hall closet.

As Beany was squeezing through Scamp's little
door, he bumped his head, snagged his sweater,
and dropped the shovel on his foot.

"Come on!" called Scamp. "You will never find anything just standing there!"

Beany hurried after Scamp, but not without thinking that they were off to a very bad start.

"We must first find a tree with bright red leaves,"
said Scamp, looking closely at the map. "I drew
the tree here to mark the spot."

"Scamp," cried Beany, "the fall leaves are gone.
All the trees look the same in the snow!"

"Well, I think the tree is over this way," said

Scamp, heading for a dark part of the woods.

They trudged through the snow for a long time.

All the trees were bare of leaves, and Beany was

thinking more and more of his warm bed.

"We will have to forget about the tree,"
said Scamp finally. "We will go to the next
place on the map. The field of wildflowers.
It should be simple to find the place where
the wildflowers grow."

"In the snow?" cried Beany. "Wildflowers don't
grow in the snow!"

"I did not think of that when I drew the map,"
said Scamp. "But if we go this way we will come
to the place where the wildflowers used to be."
"I think it is the other way," said Beany.
"Oh, no, I am sure it is this way," said Scamp. So
they started off again, going deeper and deeper into
the woods. They walked and walked and walked.

"It is useless to look for wildflowers that are not here," said Beany. "What is the next place on the map?"

"The river," said Scamp. "All we have to do is find the place where we like to fish."

"The river is frozen!" exclaimed Beany. "There
are no fishing places now."
But Scamp was not listening. He was already
pushing farther into the woods. Beany followed
after Scamp, but his feet ached and he was cold.
He thought of his warm bed and soft quilt.

The snow began to fall again. The woods were
dark and gloomy. The river was not in sight.
Up ahead, Scamp suddenly came to a stop.
Beany hurried to his side.

"What's wrong now?" he asked.

"I think we are lost," said Scamp with a gulp.

"I don't think we will *ever* find my nuts!"

"Nuts?" cried Beany. "What about finding our
way home? The snow has covered our tracks.
We are lost and I am freezing."

Scamp looked hard at Beany. "Something is different about you," he said. "Your sweater! No wonder you are cold. Your sweater is almost gone!"

"My sweater snagged on your door hook," said Beany. "It must have unraveled."

"Then we are not lost!" cried Scamp. "We can
follow the sweater yarn back to my door."
They started back through the woods, gathering
up the unraveled yarn as they went.

After a while, they saw a thin
stream of smoke. It was coming
from Scamp's chimney.
"If you had not thought of
following the yarn," said Beany,
"we would never have found our
way back."
"If you had not snagged your
sweater on my door," said Scamp,
"we would still be lost. But
here we are right at my doorway."

"We are back at your doorstep," said Beany,

"but we have not found your nuts."

"My doorstep!" cried Scamp. "Now I remember!
How convenient!"

"What are you talking about?" asked Beany.

"My nuts," said Scamp. "The square marked
Nuts on the map is my doorstep."

"I buried my nuts under my doorstep so that
they would be easy to find!" said Scamp.
"Yes, it is the perfect place," exclaimed Beany.
"It is only one step from your house."
Scamp pulled up the stone step, and Beany
began to dig.

The shovel thudded against something hard. They pulled up a chest filled with Scamp's shiny nuts and carried it inside. Soon the two friends sat by the fire cracking nuts and laughing and talking until late that night.

At last Beany said good-bye and hurried
home through the snow. When he finally
got into bed, he thought he had never
been so ready for a long winter's nap.